Mélanie Delon

ELIXIR

2. SPARKLE
OF SHADOWS

HEAVY METAL

To Jean-Philippe...

ELIXIR 2. Sparkle of shadows
ISBN 978 1 935351-19-1
© 2010 Mélanie Delon/ Represented by Norma Editorial, S.A.
Published in June 2010 by HEAVY METAL®

5 4 3 2

100 North Village Avenue, Suite 12,
Rockville Centre NY 11570

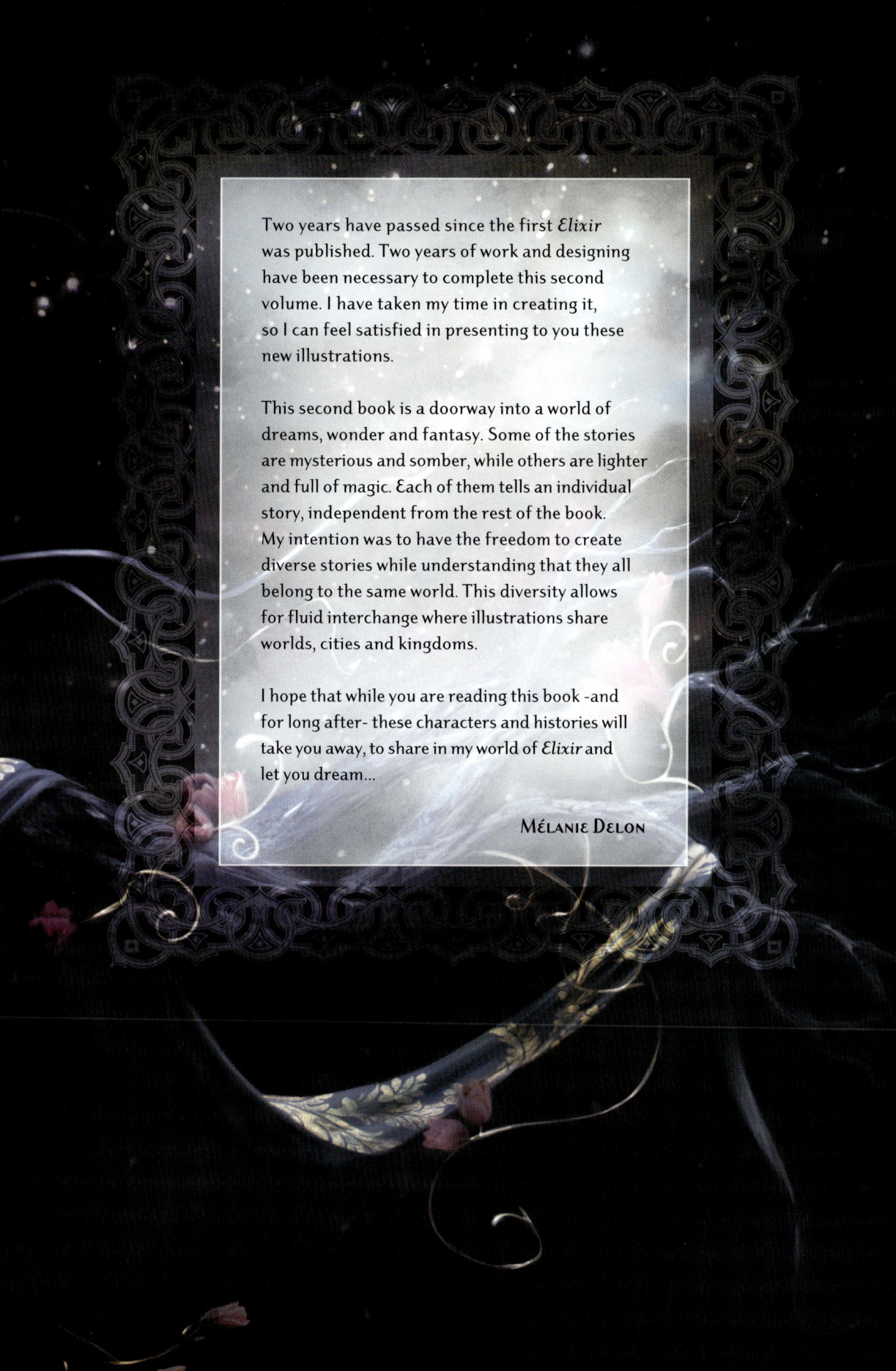

Two years have passed since the first *Elixir*
was published. Two years of work and designing
have been necessary to complete this second
volume. I have taken my time in creating it,
so I can feel satisfied in presenting to you these
new illustrations.

This second book is a doorway into a world of
dreams, wonder and fantasy. Some of the stories
are mysterious and somber, while others are lighter
and full of magic. Each of them tells an individual
story, independent from the rest of the book.
My intention was to have the freedom to create
diverse stories while understanding that they all
belong to the same world. This diversity allows
for fluid interchange where illustrations share
worlds, cities and kingdoms.

I hope that while you are reading this book -and
for long after- these characters and histories will
take you away, to share in my world of *Elixir* and
let you dream…

MÉLANIE DELON

Flower of evil 10/2009 ✞

Pain no longer exists; fear, love... they are only memories of a time past, of another me. Shadows and death are my only friends. And what I am now, you will one day become...

Enclave 10/2009 ➔

*"Spirit of the night, go, fly away,
be my eyes and my voice, and
bring comfort to the hearts of
men with my prayers."*

Black water 06/2009 ➔

The northern woods are well known as the home of the marshes. A refuge for the lost souls who bewitch and ensnare the strayed wanderers in a dreamless sleep. When they are asleep, these devilish beings take their prey to the abysses of the marsh and condemn them to live as they do after undergoing a thousand sufferings.

Chimera 03/2009 ⚓

Teremih is the essence of nature; she takes care of animals and plants. She is their mother and their protector; when one of her offspring reaches the realms of death, she accompanies them hoping that some day she will be able, if the Gods allow it, to bring them back to life.

In the snow 09/2009 ➔

Since thousands of years ago, there is a ritual performed when winter reaches its end. Nature, after falling into the trap, awaits liberation from the cold. The thawing brings with it the spark of life that will awake all the beings for the new spring.

To the east of the ashen lands there is a coast in the Boreal sea. According to the sailors, this coast is bewitched and anyone who dares go near it puts his life at risk. The people from a nearby village believe that when the storms lash out against the sea, they can hear a moan coming from that place, like someone calling, a prayer. Some people even say that the rain falling on the rocks sounds like musical notes coming from a harp.

Circe 10/2009 ⇡

Circe is the guardian of the middle
world, where the most abominable
creatures roam awaiting an order
from their mistress.

Moon 07/2008 ⇢

Cibella, known as the night light,
was the sweetest and most beautiful of
the daughters of Sahay, the port city
at the south of the empire. Her father,
an inveterate gambler, spent his time
squandering the family fortune.
With misery and hunger looming,
Cibella saw no way out, so she faced
the situation and she did something
irreparable, she murdered her father and
she took control of the family business.
But her heart was left in perpetual
mourning and her hands covered in blood.

TREASURE 06/2009 ⚲

"Light of dawn, remember us…"

WITHIN DREAMS 02/2008 →

An angel of the sun and a spirit of the
night; their love so pure that it could only
exist a few brief seconds every day: when the
sun dies down to let the moon shine, and
when the sweet light of night disappears
with the first rays of the sun.

Farewell 04/2009 ⚜

The somber days are near, the heart of men darkens,
and the forest of pure beings vainly search the light.
Norelly is one of the last descendents of her species;
she feeds on happiness, on the joy and happiness of
mankind. War is about to break out and with it all these
feelings will disappear to give way to suffering, hatred and
misfortune. And then Norelly will die with them.

Reef 06/2009 ↑

Every day, Ophelia goes to the swamps of
hope to leave some flowers as an offering.
The legend has it that the water, blessed
by the Gods, has the power to grant wishes.
Ophelia hopes to be able to make her dream
come true some day, to make her loved one
come back from the darkness...

A WINDOW
TO THE FUTURE 04/2009 ⇢

Shyë, the soothsayer, is so accomplished
at her craft that everything she predicts
becomes reality, both for good and bad:
whatever she imagines. However, her magic
only works if the other person sincerely
wants to know the future.

FATALITY 09/2008

Sally is an illegitimate
daughter; her mother was
a servant in a palace when
her master abused her.
She was thrown out of the
castle when he found out
that she was pregnant.
Sally was brought up in
misery and poverty. During
those years of hardship a
deep desire for revenge grew
within her. When she was
old enough, she managed to
be hired as a servant in the
palace and she seduced the
heir to the throne, her half
brother. Tonight she is going
to celebrate her engagement
ceremony, where she will
offer her future family
this cup full of poison.
Her vengeance will be
then fulfilled.

BEYOND BELIEF
07/2007 →

The Wind people live
past the clouds, where the
sky is at one with the stars.
They nearly never come to the
ground; their queen forbids
them from laying their feet on
firm earth. Effily respected
that rule until the day when,
alerted by a child shouting,
she went to rescue him. She
was expelled forever from
her kingdom for that act of
kindness. Then she found
herself alone, abandoned by
her kin in that hostile land...

Sleepless 04/2009 →

Ancolie's father was a man
without compassion or heart.
He starved and tortured his people.
In revenge, the witches of the
realm cast a curse on him and his
descendants. They were condemned
to live without their five senses.
He begged the witches to spare his
daughter, the only being he cared
about, from the curse, but they
refused. Ancolie could not bear to
live like that and she decided to end
her life. Her father, tortured by pain
and remorse, lost his mind. Since
then, he roams like a ghost through
a kingdom that was once his.

POISON

Enigmatic soul 01/2008 ⚓

"In my eyes, the reflection of your soul, on my skin the shadow of your love, in my heart the color of your voice, your tears will not burn out the days past."

Paradise lost 12/2009 ⚓

"Immortal flowers, invade the water with your blood colored perfume."

Blade 09/2009 ⚔

Leria owns an object coveted by all: "The dagger of Souls". It was forged in the ancient world, and it has the capacity of stealing the souls of its victims and delivering them to its beholder. Leria's family has owned this dagger for generations. Her father was its last guardian until his death, this morning. From now on, she will have to fulfill this task and protect the dagger from all those who want it.

MERCY 01/2009 →

Guardian of the
doors of paradise,
she comes to save the
souls who deserve to
enter the kingdom
of heaven.
The less fortunate
will continue on
their journey to the
darkness of hell.

✝ Nihaalen 09/2009

Estirh, I have served you for more than 400 years, you lived your best days during my endless reign and I do not regret that sacrifice. But even though my body resists the ravages of time, my soul is invaded and corrupted by fatigue. I hope you do not bear me any resentment. I laid my life at your feet, and tonight I take it back to put an end to it and rejoin those I loved, in the other world. I will take care of you where I am going...

⇐ River of tears 08/2009

After the death of her boyfriend, Nelly was disconsolate. Her family did not know what to do. They thought that time would do its work and bring back her *joie de vivre*. Days and weeks went by, but there was no change in her, until the day when she disappeared. For months, the whole village was looking for her, without any luck. Her parents eventually lost all hope of finding their daughter and they decided to build a statue representing the two lovers, from then on joined for eternity.

← Cythlehy 12/2009

Ever since childhood, Cythlehy has had strange dreams. In them she always finds the same person living the same tragedy. She also recognizes places she has never visited. She has been visiting the swamp of murmurs for years. She always goes to the same place where she saw that mysterious young woman, hoping to find out why she feels so close to her.

INQUISITION 11/2009 ↑

Diare is a Purple Shadow, an orphan who swore allegiance on her 12th birthday and who has followed for 10 years the teachings and the training of this legendary order. There are only about a hundred of them, roaming the world in order to impose their relentless justice and to defend those who cannot defend themselves.

TASTE THE DAY 04/2008 →

Yrthis reigns in the southern empire. She controls the only sea route connecting two continents. The Oracles foretold that she would meet a terrible end and that her life would be full of suffering. Unwilling to believe them, she sentenced them all to death. Since that day, their lost souls have visited her every night.

Through the mist 08/2009 →

Transformed into a nymph years ago by an evil spirit, Auralia sings to protect the fishermen and the boats that cross her territory. She tries to calm the waters and to contain the storms and the winds to allow their crossing.

Brysehii 09/2008 ⚓

Brysehii was a young girl born to a poor family. Her parents hoped that her beauty would allow her to improve her position in the world, gaining access to a better life. But reality turned out to be very different. Brysehii was wild and indomitable; she did not want a loveless marriage for money. She did not care how she earned her living. She decided to join a circus displaying freaks of nature every night. In order to be accepted she had to ravage her angel face. She accepted the sacrifice and she became the most acclaimed artist of the company.

Spirits 03/2008 ⚓

In the heart of the wasteland, Xitlahe is the last guardian of the Dark Wisdom. This power is the root of black magic, but it is even more difficult to master and much more powerful. Many adventurers have tried to steal her power, in vain. Xitlahe took an oath to surrender her own life, if necessary, to protect this wisdom.

LUCIOLE 02/2009 ⚜

Years ago, a sorcerer cast a curse on the city of Chey. He condemned its inhabitants to never again see the light of the sun. Elize was the only one who was free from this curse. Nobody knew why and, despite her investigations, she has not yet found an answer. Tomorrow she leaves for Vohonir, with the hope of finding someone there who might help her...

FEAR 03/2009 ⚔

Orthian, the goddess of war, is elusive like the wind, whispering into the ears of men so that they will develop thirst for blood and wish for death.

⚔ TEARS OF FIRE 07/2009

"My city, my house, my family are only flickering flames... Because of me, all those I love will die. May the gods forgive me some day and may my tears scorch me eternally."

VELVET 07/2009 ⚓

In the entrails of the Mountain of Silence, in the heart of the black lands lives Ystha, an old priestess of the shadows who has chosen seclusion in order to become one with her art. She is dedicated to controlling fire, and she becomes stronger every day. The day will come when she will release her rage on all those who betrayed her in her old life.

✝ RELEASE 11/2009

Far from civilization, where the forest becomes inaccessible mountains, there is a legend: hundreds of years ago, a black magic Oracle tried to reach power. She had no compassion, and she had no qualms in torturing and killing all those who dared to get in her way. Her power was such that no man or army was capable of stopping her. The witches of that ancient realm joined their forces and managed to enclose her soul in a chest that they hid where no one could find it. This box contains the darkest thing in the world and it should not be opened under any circumstance. It was hidden and bolted for centuries, far from everyone, until one day...

"Divine light, come and purify this land tainted by blood and cries. Bring wisdom and peace to the heart of the survivors. Have pity on men, they were blinded by folly."

← Eternity 07/2009

In the depths of the ocean live the people of the sea. They never wander near the surface and avoid the coasts at all costs. They do not like humans and they have no contact with them. Ohlia shares this opinion but she is more adventurous than most of her people. She spends her time in wait for a ship to founder, in order to capture the sailors while they are still alive, and to take them with her deep into the abysses until they exhale their final breath.

↑ Hocus pocus 11/2007

Amaly was raised in the streets. Since an early age she has had magical powers, like controlling animals, or bending the will of the weakest souls. One day, one of the sorcerers of the city noticed her, took her under his protection and transmitted his wisdom to her. She improved daily, until she eventually surpassed her master. He then understood that Amaly was not like the other girls, and that her mysterious origins probably belied a terrible secret. He then sent her to the Tower of Shadows, the center of magic, to discover the truth...

Nemesis 11/2007 ☥

This is Illeys, an actress. Saul, her lover, is a theatrical director. They have spent the last two years setting up their theatre. Illeys is a success on stage and Saul's penmanship knows no equal.
But with their greatest piece, the one that will cement their reputations in the trade, Saul suddenly decides to give the lead role to a young actress, whose only talent is undressing on stage.
Tonight is the opening night. Illeys, blinded by revenge, will invoke all the dark powers and magic that will bring chaos and misfortune to the theatre...

DISTURBED 05/2009 ⚓

A demonic spirit bent on poisoning and on sowing the earth with the most deadly diseases. She knows no compassion, and she can strike against any town or village without leaving any survivors, other than decrepitude and death.

In the roofs of Vahonir, Tesry, a little girl who sells fruit and plays the violin on the streets, takes refuge for the night, while the city sleeps and it becomes an ocean of stars. Lately, she is not the only spectator of the landscape of the night. A strange creature that seems straight from her childhood stories has appeared. Where did it come from and what is it doing here?

COLD BLOODED 12/2009 ⚔

Poison runs through her veins, vengeance has taken over her heart.
Syrha is the most wanted assassin in the realm. Until now, no one has been able
to unmask her; she travels city to city spreading death in her wake. What is
she hiding behind her darkness and what is the motivation for so much evil?

TEMPTATION 11/2009 →

Her husband has abandoned her, taking with him their only
daughter. The pain that this separation from her daughter
brings is unbearable and Theresa, surrounded by the hubris of
her former life, slowly sinks into desperation and madness.

Biography

Mélanie Delon was born in 1980 in a small village outside of Paris, France. She was naturally creative from an early age with a particular fondness for drawing. After discovering and mastering 2D digital software in 2005 she began her career in illustration. Since then Mélanie has developed her own personal world revolving around themes and characters inspired by a mix of classicism, romanticism and fantasy. Mélanie has worked for many international publishers including Penguin, Random House, HaperCollins and Macmillan. She also works in the video game industry and contributes work to magazines specializing in digital art including *Imagine FX*.

Mélanie's work can also been seen featured in illustration books and collections including *Exotique* (#2, #3, and #5), *Expose* (#4, #5, and #7) published by Ballistic Publishing as well as in *Spectrum* (#14, #15, and #16 including the cover). She is also the co-author of *D'artiste Digital Painting 2* (Ballistic Publishing). Mélanie's first art book, *Elixir: In Silence* was published in 2007 by Norma Editorial.